This
Harry and
the
Dinosaurs
book belongs to

. . . .

SCELIDOSAURUS

(ske-LI-doh-SAW-rus)

TYRANNOSAURUS

(tie-RAN-oh-SAW-rus)

TRICERATOPS

(try-SER-a-tops)

STEGOSAURUS

(STEG-oh-SAW-rus)

PTERODACTYL

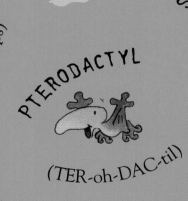

(TER-oh-DAC-til)

APATOSAURUS

(a-PAT-oh-SAW-rus)

ANCHISAURUS

(AN-ki-SAW-rus)

SCELIDOSAURUS

(ske-LI-doh-SAW-rus)

TYRANNOSAURUS

(tie-RAN-oh-SAW-rus)

TRICERATOPS

(try-SER-a-tops)

PTERODACTYL

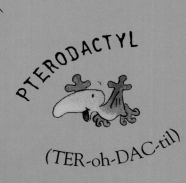

(TER-oh-DAC-til)

STEGOSAURUS

(STEG-oh-SAW-rus)

APATOSAURUS

(a-PAT-oh-SAW-rus)

ANCHISAURUS

(AN-ki-SAW-rus)

PUFFIN BOOKS
Published by the Penguin Group: London, New York, Australia, Canada, India, Ireland, New Zealand and South Africa
Penguin Books Ltd, Registered Offices: 80 Strand, London WC2R 0RL, England

puffinbooks.com

Harry and the Bucketful of Dinosaurs first published by David & Charles Children's Books 1999; published in Puffin Books 2003
Harry and the Dinosaurs go to School first published in Puffin Books 2006
Harry and the Dinosaurs make a Splash first published in Puffin Books 2007
This collection first published 2011

001 – 10 9 8 7 6 5 4 3 2 1

ISBN: 978–0–141–34283–2

Adventures with Harry and the Bucketful of Dinosaurs

Ian Whybrow **Adrian Reynolds**

PUFFIN

Contents

For Thomas Owlett
who introduced his bucketful of dinosaurs
to Ann and me one lucky Sunday afternoon
at The Chelsea Gardener
I.W.

For William
A.R.

With thanks to Dr Angela Milner
at the Natural History Museum, London

Harry and the Bucketful of Dinosaurs

Ian Whybrow Adrian Reynolds

PUFFIN

Nan thought the attic needed a clear out.
She let Harry help.
Harry found an old box
all grey with dust.

He lifted the lid . . .
DINOSAURS!

Harry took the
dinosaurs downstairs.

He unbent the
bent ones.

He fixed all the
broken ones.

He got up on a chair and washed them in the sink.
Nan came to see and say, "Just what do
you think you're up to?"

"Dinosaurs don't like boxes," Harry said.
"They want to be in a bucket."

Sam came in from watching TV.
She said it was stupid, fussing over so much junk.
"Dinosaurs *aren't* junk," Harry said.

The next day, Harry went to the library with Mum.
He took the dinosaurs in their bucket.

He found out all the names in a book
and told them to the dinosaurs.
He spoke softly to each one.
He whispered,
   "You are my Scelidosaurus."
   "You are my Stegosaurus."
   "You are my Triceratops."

And there were enough names for all the Apatosauruses
and Anchisauruses and Tyrannosauruses.
The dinosaurs said, "Thank you, Harry."
They said it very quietly, but just
loud enough for Harry to hear.

Sometimes they got left behind.
But they never got lost for long because
Harry knew all their names.

And he always called out their names,
just to make sure they were safe.

One day, Harry went on a train with Nan.
He was so excited, he forgot all
about the bucket.

Nan dried his eyes.
"Never mind," she said.
"I'll buy you a nice new DVD."

Harry watched the DVD with Sam.
It was nice, but not like the dinosaurs.

At bedtime, Harry said to Mum, "I like DVDs.
But I like my dinosaurs better
because you can fix them, you can bath them,
you can take them to bed.

And best of all, you can say their names."

Harry was still upset at breakfast next morning.
Sam said, "*Dusty old junk!*"
That was why Sam's book got milk on it.
Nan took Harry to his room to settle down.

Later, Nan took Harry back to the train station to
see the Lost Property Man.
The man said, "Dinosaurs? Yes we have found some dinosaurs.
But how do we know they are *your* dinosaurs?"

Harry said, "I will close
my eyes and call their names.
Then you will know."

And Harry closed his eyes and called the names.
He called,

"Come bac

my Scelidosaurus!"

"Come back my Stegosaurus!"

"Come back my Triceratops!"

He called, 'come back', to the Apatosauruses
and the Anchisauruses
and the Tyrannosauruses
and all the lost old dinosaurs.
And when he opened his eyes . . .

. . . there they were – all of them standing on
the counter next to the bucket!
"All correct!" said the man.
"These are *definitely* your dinosaurs. Definitely!"

And the dinosaurs whispered to Harry.
They whispered very quietly, but
just loud enough for Harry to hear.
They said, "You are definitely *our* Harry, definitely!"

Going home from the station,
Harry held the bucket very tight.
Nan said to the neighbour, "Our Harry
likes those old dinosaurs."

"*Definitely*," whispered Harry.
"And my dinosaurs definitely like me!"
ENDOSAURUS

In memory of Mason Jones and for all of his friends
at Deri Primary School, Bargoed, who miss him very much - I.W.

For Calum - A.R.

Harry and the Dinosaurs
go to School

Ian Whybrow **Adrian Reynolds**

PUFFIN

It was a big day for Harry. He was starting at his new school.
He was very excited because one of his friends, Charlie,
was starting that day too.

Stegosaurus said he didn't want to go. Not after
Triceratops told him about no Raaahs in class.
Mum said not to worry, school would be fine.

Harry blew his whistle just like a teacher.
    He said, "In twos, holding hands, my dinosaurs.
No talking and jump in the bucket."

The dinosaurs did what Harry said.
    All except Stegosaurus. He was so
nervous, all his plates were rattling.
    Harry had to give him a special stroke.

Sam said, "You can't take dinosaurs to school, stupid!"
That's why her toast fell on the floor.

Mum took Harry to school.

Mrs Rance was waiting at the classroom door when
Harry and Mum got there.
"Hello, Harry," she said. "Welcome to your new school."
They all said goodbye to the mums and dads.

Then Mrs Rance showed Harry the coat pegs.
"You can leave your lunchbox here too," she said.
Harry was too shy to say could he have his bucket back.
That's why his dinosaurs got left outside the classroom.

Harry missed his dinosaurs, so he didn't like the classroom. He didn't like the home corner, or his special work tray.

And he felt sorry for another new boy with a digger
who cried when his mum went home.
  The boy wouldn't say one single word, not even his name.

Harry sort of liked the playground at playtime.
But it wasn't much fun, even the monkey bars –
not without his dinosaurs.

Back in class, the digger boy still wouldn't speak.
  "Maybe he wants to go to the toilet," Harry suggested.
"I'll show him where it is, shall I?"
  Mrs Rance said good idea, how thoughtful.

All the way to the toilet the boy kept quiet.
  It was the same on the way back, till they got to the coats.
Then they heard a voice, very sad and very soft.
  "Raaaaaaaaaah!" it said.

"That's my dinosaurs," said Harry. "They miss me.
Would you like to see them?"
    The boy nodded so Harry said, "This is my Apatosaurus
and my Anchisaurus and my Scelidosaurus.

This is Triceratops and Tyrannosaurus. Pterodactyl is the baby. Wait! Where's Stegosaurus?"

"Jump out, Stegosaurus," called Harry. "Don't be shy!"

But Stegosaurus wanted a whisper.

"Ah," said Harry. "Stegosaurus says he will come out but only if he can have a ride on your digger."

And do you know what? The boy nodded and passed it over.

When Harry and the boy got back, Mrs Rance said,
"Oh good! Dinosaurs. I love dinosaurs. Do they Raaah?"

"RAAAAAAAAAAAAAAH!" said the dinosaurs
and blew all the windows open.
   "My goodness!" said Mrs Rance. "That *was* a Raaah!"

They all sat down in the classroom.
  "Now, we're going to make new labels for our coat pegs," said Mrs Rance. "Hands up who knows how to write their name?"

The boy with the digger put up his hand.
"And what are you going to write?" smiled Mrs Rance.
"Jackosaurus!" said the boy.
It was the very first word he had spoken all day.
And what a good joke, too!
All the other children laughed and laughed.

Harry felt very happy.
 Charlie, Harry and their new friend Jack sat down together at a table with the dinosaurs.

They laughed and they Raaahed
and they made beautiful labels
to show where they belonged.

ENDOSAURUS

Three Raaaahs for Cosmo, Albie and Circe,
the wee Millers of Holmeknowe! – I.W.

For Luciana Olivia Linciano – A.R.

Harry and the Dinosaurs

make a Splash

Ian Whybrow Adrian Reynolds

PUFFIN

Harry and the dinosaurs loved the wave pool at the indoor Water World. Jumping over the waves with Sam was FUN!

Then a big wave came and knocked them all over!
That spoiled it! That wasn't nice at all. The water
made them cough and got in their eyes.

"Raaah!" said Anchisaurus. "This tastes terrible, Harry!"

"Raaah!" said Triceratops. "Our bath at home is much nicer!"

"Quick," said Scelidosaurus. "Let's run away!"

So Harry and the dinosaurs ran back to Nan.
  "Why don't you come in this pool?"
she said, but they didn't want to.
  "Raaah! We hate water now,"
said Tyrannosaurus.

Nan said, "What a shame them old
waves spoiled things for you. Let's see
if something cool will help."

She took them for some juice and double scoops of ice cream with extra sticky stuff. Ahhh! That helped a lot!

"Are you ready to go swimming again now, Harry?" asked Nan.

Harry wasn't sure. "My dinosaurs don't like getting splashed," he said. "But maybe they'll go in if you come too, Nan."

Nan looked worried.

"I'm ever so sorry," she said. "I haven't been swimming for years. I expect I should sink like a stone!"

Sam said it was stupid coming all this way and then being too scared to go in.

That was why Nan threw a bucket of water over her.

"Mind your own business, Miss Cleverstick!" she shouted.

Harry took Nan to settle down.

"You're not allowed to splash people in swimming pools, Nan!" he told her.

Nan said quite right, shocking, she was ashamed of herself.

So Harry and the dinosaurs took her to watch
the people on the water slide.
    Nan thought that looked tree-mendous!
    "Why don't you try that, Harry?" she said.
"Sam would take you, I'm sure."

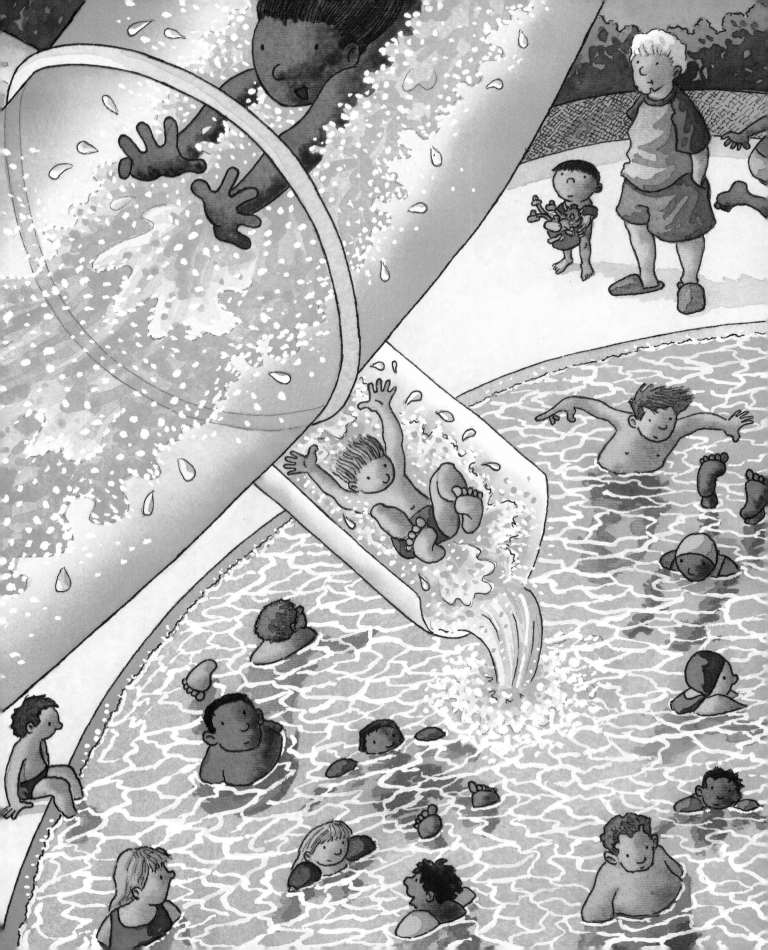

It *did* look really fun, but Harry and the dinosaurs didn't feel *quite* brave enough yet.

"Raaah!" said Apatosaurus. "We don't want to go with Sam!"

"We only want to go with you, Nan," said Harry.

"That's ever so high . . ." said Nan. "But I suppose we'll be all right if we stick together!"

She grabbed Harry's hand and they rushed off to the shop.
Nan chose a bright yellow swimsuit for herself and some
goggles for Harry.

"Here, pop these on," said Nan, "while I buy myself some
senior armbands."

"Let's go!" said the dinosaurs. "If Nan
can do it, we can do it!"
They climbed right up to the top and
they were only a little bit scared.

What a surprise for Sam!
Nan and Harry and the dinosaurs
made the biggest SPLASH of the day!

"Cool!" laughed Sam. "And I thought you
you were scared of the water."
"I was nervous, that's all," said Nan.
"But Harry's helping me."
"And my dinosaurs!" said Harry.
"They're helping too!"

"Raaah!" said Pterodactyl. "I'm a dive bomber!"
"We like rough waves now," said Scelidosaurus.
"Look, we can bite them!"

"How do I look?" laughed Nan. "Am I sinking like a stone?"
"No, you're definitely swimming!" said Harry and the
dinosaurs. "You look tree-mendous!"

ENDOSAURUS

SCELIDOSAURUS

(ske-LI-doh-SAW-rus)

TYRANNOSAURUS

(tie-RAN-oh-SAW-rus)

TRICERATOPS

(try-SER-a-tops)

PTERODACTYL

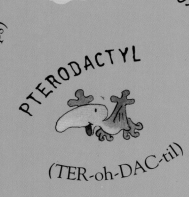

(TER-oh-DAC-til)

STEGOSAURUS

(STEG-oh-SAW-rus)

APATOSAURUS

(a-PAT-oh-SAW-rus)

ANCHISAURUS

(AN-ki-SAW-rus)

SCELIDOSAURUS

(ske-LI-doh-SAW-rus)

TYRANNOSAURUS

(tie-RAN-oh-SAW-rus)

TRICERATOPS

(try-SER-a-tops)

PTERODACTYL

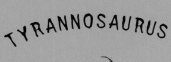

(TER-oh-DAC-til)

STEGOSAURUS

(STEG-oh-SAW-rus)

APATOSAURUS

(a-PAT-oh-SAW-rus)

ANCHISAURUS

(AN-ki-SAW-rus)